# EXTRAORDINARY
## WARREN

## SAVES THE DAY

### by Sarah Dillard

ALADDIN

New York  London  Toronto  Sydney  New Delhi

ALADDIN

An imprint of Simon & Schuster Children's Publishing Division

1230 Avenue of the Americas, New York, NY 10020

First Aladdin paper-over-board edition October 2014

Copyright © 2014 by Sarah Dillard

All rights reserved, including the right of reproduction in whole or in part in any form.

ALADDIN is a trademark of Simon & Schuster, Inc., and related logo is a registered trademark of Simon & Schuster, Inc.

For information about special discounts for bulk purchases, please contact Simon & Schuster Special Sales at 1-866-506-1949 or business@simonandschuster.com.

The Simon & Schuster Speakers Bureau can bring authors to your live event. For more information or to book an event contact the Simon & Schuster Speakers Bureau at 1-866-248-3049 or visit our website at www.simonspeakers.com.

Designed by Laura Lyn DiSiena

The text of this book was set in Carnes Handscript and Jacoby.

The illustrations for this book were rendered digitally.

Manufactured in China 0714 SCP

10 9 8 7 6 5 4 3 2 1

This book has been cataloged with the Library of Congress.

ISBN 978-1-4814-0352-8

ISBN 978-1-4814-0353-5 (eBook)

For the Malick chicks...
Juliet
&
Eloise

# CHAPTER 1

Warren was a chicken who lived
on a small farm.

Most days, Warren and the
other chickens pecked and peeped,
peeped and pecked.

But then Coach Stanley made a few changes
to their daily routine.

From sunup until sundown, the chicks
were busy.

They danced.

They stretched.

They sang.

Warren liked all the new activities.
He especially enjoyed nap time.

He dreamed of all the faraway places he would visit someday.

Warren's naps never lasted long enough.

All the chicks thought Warren was hilarious.

No one took Warren seriously, except for...

# CHAPTER

Egg.

Egg had recently hatched, and Warren had taken him under his wing.

# He answered Egg's endless questions.

Warren taught Egg everything he knew.

☆Listen to Coach.  ☆Never trust a rat.
☆The early bird catches the worm.
☆The moon is made of green cheese.
☆Always follow the brightest star.
☆If at first you don't succeed,
try, try again.

11

That night while the other chickens slept,

Egg thought
about flying,

and Warren thought
about the moon.

# CHAPTER ③

The next morning, Egg woke up before everyone else.

He was determined to fly.

That didn't work.

Egg tried and he tried.

One more time
he jumped,

flapped, and...

flew!

He landed on the other side of the road.

First he found…

Then he discovered…

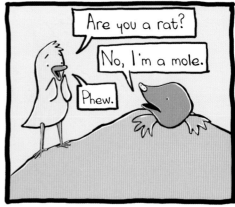

Egg kept exploring until he was in the middle of...

a jungle!

I'm really seeing the world!

I've got to go home and tell Warren!

But when Egg turned to leave,
he wasn't sure which way to go.

# CHAPTER 4

When Warren woke up, he was still thinking
about the moon. He thought about it all day.

At breakfast.

At exercise class.

At nap time.

During gymnastics, he told the chicks his plans.

But after lunch, during their weekly
game of hide-and-seek, Warren was all business.

It was finally his turn to be "IT."

Warren found everyone,
except for...

Warren searched high and low,
inside and out,
and all around the farm.

But Egg was nowhere
to be found.

That left one last
place to look.

# Millard's trash can.

33

Warren ran all the way to the side of the road.
Then he stopped.

Warren knew he
had no choice.

He looked to the left.
He looked to the
right. And...

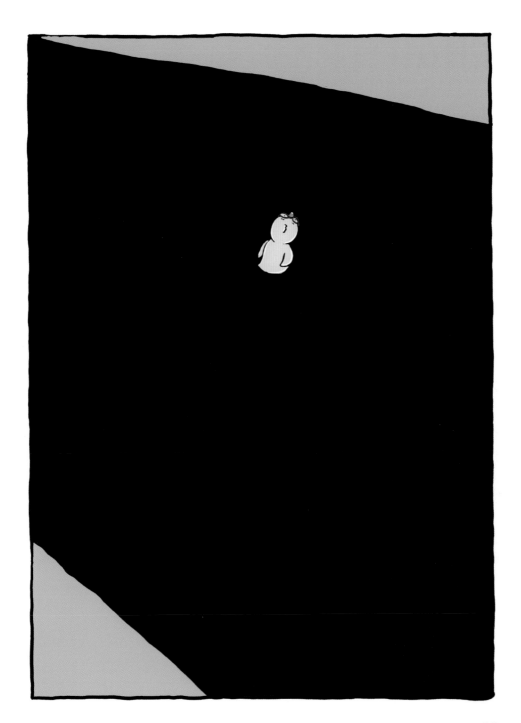

# CHAPTER 5

On the other side of the road, Warren spotted a cow.

He raced away as fast as he could,

past the pond,

the molehill,

deep into the cornfield,

until he was out of breath.

And then he
remembered.

# CHAPTER

Back at the barnyard, the chickens were
singing the last song of the day.

The chicks scurried to
find Coach Stanley.

Immediately, the chicks started decorating.

They made so much noise, they woke up...

# MILLARD.

# CHAPTER 7

Warren looked high and low, but Egg was nowhere to be found.
It was getting dark, and a little bit cold, and he wasn't sure what to do next.

Egg is probably hungry. And lonely. And sleepy. And scared.

He doesn't know as much about the world as I do.

But then Warren heard a familiar voice.

# But it wasn't so easy after all.

Egg—that's it!

And there's the star! Let's go!

Warren and Egg followed the light of
the star across the road and home,

just as Millard was crossing
in the other direction.

# CHAPTER 8

When Warren and Egg reached the farm,
the search party was in full swing.

Egg told everyone about their adventures.

There was a cow!

And mountains!

And the ocean!

We were in a jungle.

We met a spider.

Oh, and I flew.

Warren taught me!

The chicks thought Egg was hilarious.

Warren

taught him

to fly. HAH!

Peep!

They laughed all the way to bed.

o  o

Egg flew? Nah. It couldn't be.

But Warren and Egg weren't quite ready to go to sleep.

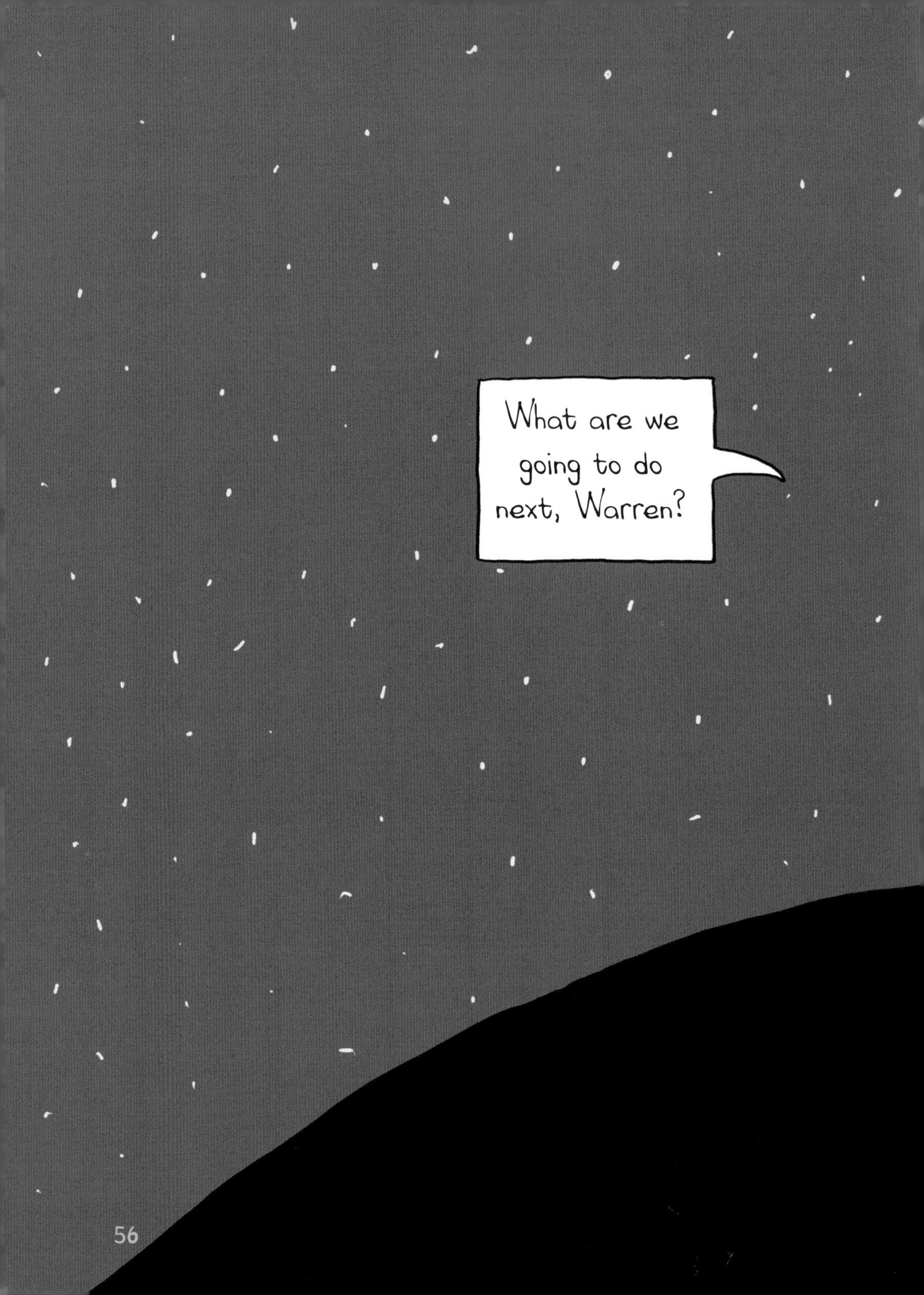
What are we going to do next, Warren?

Meanwhile, on the other side
of the road...

MooOOVe it!

**Sarah Dillard** grew up in a small town in Massachusetts. She studied art and English literature at Wheaton College, and illustration at the Rhode Island School of Design. She lives on a mountain in Vermont with her husband and dog, both of whom inspire many of her characters, and ensure that she goes for a walk every day. You can visit Sarah online at sarahdillard.com.